Happy Reading!

Ann Mullen

I Love Birds

Written by Ann Miller
Illustration by Kevin Duffy

Jaylil Publishing Company

Library of Congress Cataloging-in-Publication Data

Jaylil Publishing Company
Post Office Box 656551
Flushing, New York 11365

ISBN 0-9748165-0-7

Printed in Korea

For:
Raia
Amber
Asa
Aria
and You,_____.

Love, your Grand

I love birds! All kinds of birds.

1

Red ones and black ones, yellow ones and blue ones!

2

I watch them through my window.

I peek at them through my door.

4

I even watch them lying on the floor.

I watch them as they fly from the trees.

6

Sometimes to get a better look, I get down on my knees.

I love birds, they are one of my favorite things.

8

They make me happy, when they sing.

I think it's funny, when they walk on the ground.

10

Once I saw some from the car, as we drove to town.

I love birds! All kinds of birds.

Red ones and black ones, yellow ones and blue ones.

Sometimes I feed them.

Sometimes I shoo them.

Sometimes they let me walk right up to them!

I love birds, you can believe what I say.

I can play with them all through the day.

I see birds everywhere I go.

I love birds! All kinds of birds.

Big ones and small ones, short ones and tall ones.

Red ones and black ones, yellow ones and blue ones.

23

About the birds in this book.

Throughout this book, we have drawn many different types of birds from around the world and from right in your back yard.

Please use this reference to identify the birds in this book.

(Starting in the top left of the page and moving clockwise.)

PAGE 1 - Flamingo, Canadian geese, green parrot, humming bird, seagull, mallard (duck)

PAGE 2 - Cardinal, raven, blue jay, yellow finch

PAGE 12. - Bald eagle, vulture, brown pelican, robin, bantam rooster, great horned owl

PAGE 13 - Red parrot, puffin, great blue heron, duckling

PAGE 21 - Toucan, green honeycreeper (on log), scarlet ibis (directly above and below log), stork (in water), emu, kiwi (beneath toucan)

PAGE 22 - Turkey, black-capped chickadee, ostrich, emperor penguin

PAGE 23 - Pine grosbeak, cormorant, peacock, eastern meadowlark

How many birds can you name on each of these pages?

3_____

4_____

5_____

6_____

7_____

8_____

9_____

10_____

11_____

14_____

15_____

16_____

17_____

18_____

19_____

20_____

About the Author

Ann Miller is a mother and grandmother. It's been one of her lifelong dreams to write and publish children's books. This is the first in a series of I love animals books. Ann has a bachelors degree in Business Administration and a Masters in Social Science. She works as the Director of Patient Financial Services in a Brooklyn, New York hospital. She resides in Queens, New York.

About the Illustrator

Kevin Duffy grew up in Winchester, MA and has been drawing cartoons since he was a kid. He decided to end a successful career in publishing in 1997 to follow his passion for cartooning full-time. Since that time, his cartoons have appeared in magazines, newspapers and on the Web. He has illustrated several books including *Let's Just Take This Outside, Nuts in the Woodwork,* and *Utah or Bust.* He is also the creator of the cartoon Virtual Humor. Kevin lives in southern NH with his wife, daughter, and son. For more information about Kevin and his cartoons visit his Web site at www.kevinduffy.net.